090148

Z   Zelver, Patricia
         The wedding of Don Octavio.

090148

on Octavio.

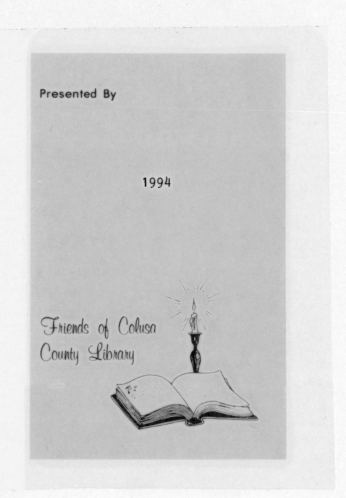

THE·WEDDING·OF
DON·OCTAVIO

THE · WEDDING ·

by Patricia Zelver

OF·DON·OCTAVIO

pictures by Larry Daste

TAMBOURINE BOOKS   NEW YORK

13.93

94B5598

Library of Congress Cataloging in Publication Data

Zelver, Patricia. The wedding of Don Octavio / Patricia Zelver;
illustrated by Larry Daste.   p.   cm.
Summary: Don Octavio feeds his animal friends every day,
but they fear that he will forget about them
when he marries the Lady of the Laughing Eyes.
[1. Animals—Fiction.   2. Weddings—Fiction.]
I. Daste, Larry, ill.   II. Title.
PZ7.Z399We   1993   [E]—dc20.   92-12587   CIP   AC
ISBN 0-688-11334-6.—ISBN 0-688-11335-4 (lib. bdg.)
1 3 5 7 9 10 8 6 4 2
FIRST EDITION

For Aida   P. Z.

To Mom and Dad..."Always"   L.D.

Don Octavio, poet, widower, and friend to animals, lived in
a little adobe casa in a small village on the edge of a jungle
in the shadow of a great volcano.

Don Octavio was a man of regular habits. Every morning he rose at dawn and went out on his patio to greet the sun.

Then he fed his beloved pets. He gave a handful of seeds to Carlota, the green and orange parrot, a banana to Paco, the spider monkey, and a bone to Señor Gonzales, the yellow dog. El Tigre, the cat, got a bowl of warm goat's milk, and Violeta, the burro, a pail of oats. Don Sinuoso, the boa constrictor, was especially fond of raw eggs.

After this Don Octavio dressed for the day. He ate a sliced orange prepared by Josefina, his housekeeper, and picked a bachelor button for his buttonhole.

Then he hopped on his bicycle and rode into the village to the steps of the church, where he sat at a little table and read and wrote letters for people who did not know how to read or write.

At exactly two o'clock Don Octavio rode home. He ate his midday meal then retired to his salón, where he wrote his daily poem. All the animals knew they must be very quiet while he worked.

At dusk, Don Octavio went into his garden, stood under the sapodilla tree and recited his new poem with all the animals gathered about him.

In the evening, Don Octavio ate a simple supper, climbed into his bed, and slept soundly until daybreak.

Then, one day—things changed. It was Carlota who first noticed that Don Octavio was not himself.

"He doesn't eat," said Carlota. "He takes a bite of his tamale, then pushes the plate away."

"He gave my banana to Violeta and he gave El Tigre's milk to me," said Paco.

Everyone agreed that the most disturbing change of all was Don Octavio's poetry. He no longer wrote about the good familiar things the animals understood. Instead, he addressed his poems to a strange lady. The Lady of the Laughing Eyes, he called her.

"Our master must be sick," cried Carlota.

"He should see a doctor," said Paco.

Then El Tigre spoke. "You are all wrong," he said. "Don Octavio is not sick. It's even worse than that. Don Octavio is in love. I heard him talking to Josefina. He is in love with the Lady of the Laughing Eyes and they are to be married on Sunday."

"Married?" shrieked Carlota.

"She probably won't even let us in the house," groaned Violeta.

"He has forgotten us!" Paco cried.

The day of the wedding arrived. A carriage appeared at the door and Don Octavio, splendid in a striped suit, seated himself in the back. Sadly, the animals watched him leave.

"When he comes back," said Carlota, "he will bring her."

"Our new mistress," sighed Señor Gonzales.

"Nothing will ever be the same again," said Paco, weeping big tears.

Out on the patio Josefina strung paper lanterns and crepe paper on the sapodilla tree and she covered a table with the best lace cloth. An old man and his son delivered a basket of fireworks and the marimba band marched in. Last of all Josefina brought out the wedding cake. Paco's mouth watered when he saw it, but Josefina shooed him away.

"Don't think we'll get any," El Tigre said to him. "Nobody's thinking of us."

Poor Paco. He climbed the sapodilla tree and dangled there, staring greedily at the cake below.

At that moment the band struck up the wedding march and in came Don Octavio with the Lady of the Laughing Eyes on his arm. Friends and relatives lined up to kiss the bride. A photographer asked the bride to pose, cutting the cake. She had just lifted the knife when poor Paco, overcome by the cake's delicious smell, lost his balance and fell head first into the frosting. The band stopped playing. Everyone was silent.

"We're done for now," Don Sinuoso whispered to Violeta, and he slithered away under the table to hide.

Just then the Lady laughed!

"Oh, what a dear little monkey," she cried. She plucked Paco out of the cake and brushed him off and cuddled him in her arms. Then she saw Carlota. "What a beautiful parrot," the Lady said. Carlota spread her feathers and preened. She petted Señor Gonzales and El Tigre and kissed Violeta on her wet nose.

Now it was Don Sinuoso's turn. He slid out from
under the table and stretched out his great length to
be admired.

"I have never seen such a noble snake," said the Lady.

"I think I like this Lady of the Laughing Eyes," Don
Sinuoso said to himself.

The photographer prepared to take the photograph
again.

"Wait. Please," the Lady said. She arranged the
animals around her.

"Don't forget Don Octavio," somebody called out.
The wedding guests laughed. Don Octavio took his place
beside his bride and the photographer snapped the picture.

The band began to play a lively waltz.

Then Don Octavio stood under the sapodilla tree and recited his new poem in honor of the wedding. The old man and the little boy shot off fireworks and everyone cheered.

That day Paco ate so much wedding cake he thought he would burst.
That night the Lady of the Laughing Eyes rubbed his stomach and sang him to sleep.